For Bill, who loves the
garden!
—A.S.C.

I Can Read® and I Can Read Book® are trademarks of HarperCollins Publishers.
Biscuit and Friends Visit the Community Garden
Text copyright © 2022 by Alyssa Satin Capucilli. Illustrations copyright © 2022 by Pat Schories.
All rights reserved. Printed in the United States of America.
No part of this book may be used or reproduced in any manner whatsoever without written permission except
in the case of brief quotations embodied in critical articles and reviews. For information address HarperCollins
Children's Books, a division of HarperCollins Publishers, 195 Broadway, New York, NY 10007.
www.icanread.com

Library of Congress Control Number: 2021943589
ISBN 978-0-06-291001-1 (trade bdg.)—ISBN 978-0-06-291000-4 (pbk.)

Book design by Chrisila Maida
                      22 23 24 25 26   LSCC   10 9 8 7 6 5 4 3 2 1   ❖   First Edition

Biscuit
and Friends

VISIT THE COMMUNITY GARDEN

story by ALYSSA SATIN CAPUCILLI
pictures by ROSE MARY BERLIN
in the style of PAT SCHORIES

HARPER

An Imprint of HarperCollinsPublishers

Seeds—check!

Shovel—check!

Watering can—check!

"We're going to the community garden,
Biscuit."

Woof, woof!

Biscuit was ready to explore

as soon as they arrived!

"Stay with me, Biscuit,"
said the little girl.
"The community garden is a big
and busy place."

Biscuit saw rows and rows of plants.

He saw people digging!

Woof!

Could Biscuit dig, too?

"No digging yet, Biscuit,"
said the little girl.
"First, let's find our friends."

Just then, Biscuit heard

a familiar sound.

Bow wow! Bow wow!

Who could that be?

"You found our friends, Biscuit,"
said the little girl.
"Now we can all help in the garden."
Everyone found a shovel or a rake.

14

Puddles found a worm wiggling

in the soil.

Biscuit found a tiny bird.

15

Woof, woof!

Did the bird want to play?

Biscuit chased the tiny bird.

Biscuit jumped and jumped.

He landed with a big thump.

Birdseed flew everywhere!

Woof!

Biscuit hurried back to find his friends.
On the way, he saw a woman busy
tugging.

Woof, woof!

Biscuit loved to tug and pull!

"You sure know how to tug!"

she said.

Biscuit continued on his way.

He saw brightly colored flowers.

He saw a sprinkler, too.

Woof, woof!

Biscuit ran and splashed.

He gave a big shake.

The water flew all around!

Woof, woof!

Now Biscuit walked up and down

the garden rows.

Where could his friends be?

Biscuit found chipmunks and squirrels.

He even found a lost teddy bear.

Biscuit returned it right away!

Biscuit had just seen a butterfly

when the little girl said,

"There you are, silly puppy!"

Oh, Biscuit. Where have you been?"

But then some gardeners asked,

"Is this your puppy, little girl?"

Woof, woof!

"Your puppy
helped me feed
the birds!"

"He helped me
pull the carrots."

"He helped me
water the plants!"

"Your puppy found my teddy bear.
I hope you'll bring him again."

Woof, woof!

"Funny puppy!

You made lots of friends

and helped in the garden today.

There's still time for digging. . . .

And time to meet another friend, too!"

Hop, hop!

Woof, woof!